Katie Woo's

❋ Neighborhood ❋

Mr. Patel Builds

by Fran Manushkin

illustrated by Laura Zarrin

PICTURE WINDOW BOOKS
a capstone imprint

EREADER
MANUSHKI

Katie Woo's Neighborhood is published by
Picture Window Books, an imprint of Capstone.
1710 Roe Crest Drive
North Mankato, Minnesota 56003
www.capstonepub.com

Text © 2021 Fran Manushkin
Illustrations © 2021 Picture Window Books

Library of Congress Cataloging-in-Publication Data
Names: Manushkin, Fran, author. | Zarrin, Laura, illustrator.
Title: Mr. Patel builds / by Fran Manushkin; illustrated by Laura Zarrin.
Description: North Mankato, Minnesota : Picture Window Books, a
Capstone imprint, [2021] | Series: Katie Woo's neighborhood | Audience:
Ages 5–7. | Audience: Grades K–1. |
Summary: Katie's class is invited to see a new house a classmate's father
is building, where they learn the steps to building a house and even who
the new homeowner is. Includes glossary, discussion questions, and an
interview.
Identifiers: LCCN 2020025182 (print) | LCCN 2020025183 (ebook) |
ISBN 9781515882398 (library binding) | ISBN 9781515883487 (trade
paperback) | ISBN 9781515892137 (pdf)
Subjects: CYAC: Dwellings—Design and construction—Fiction. |
Building—Fiction. | Schools—Fiction. | Chinese Americans—Fiction.
Classification: LCC PZ7.M3195 Mr 2021 (print) | LCC PZ7.M3195 (ebook)
| DDC [E]—dc23
LC record available at https://lccn.loc.gov/2020025182
LC ebook record available at https://lccn.loc.gov/2020025183

$15.99

Designer: Bobbie Nuytten

AUG - 21

2

Table of Contents

Katie's Neighborhood

Police

Library

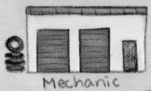

Mechanic

City Hall

Grocery Store

Post Office

School

Chapter 1

Learning About Houses

Miss Winkle told Katie's

class, "Today we will learn

how to build a house."

"Cool!" said Katie. "We

all need a place to live."

"I have a better idea," said
Roddy. "Let's learn how to
wreck a house. BASH! SMASH!
CRASH!"

"Wrecking a house is

too easy," said Miss Winkle.

"Building a house is hard."

Miss Winkle asked the
class, "Can you name some
kinds of houses that people
live in?"

"Igloos!" said Katie.

"Yurts!" said JoJo.

"Tepees!" yelled Pedro.

"Treehouses," said Barry.

"I have one

in my yard."

"Those are good answers!" said Miss Winkle. "Today, most of our houses are made of bricks or wood."

"My dad is a builder," said
Peter Patel. "He wants us to
watch him build a house."

Miss Winkle smiled. "It's a
special house," she said.

"I wonder why," said Katie.

Chapter 2
Building a House

The next day the class

went to see the house. Mr.

Patel said, "First we dug a

hole with a machine called

a digger."

"Then a truck filled the hole with concrete. That is the foundation."

"Right!" said Peter Patel. "It makes the house strong."

"Then it was time for

the carpenters to work," said

Mr. Patel. "They did a great

job putting up the wood."

Katie watched workers

putting shingles on the roof.

"These will keep out the

rain," said Katie. "I hate a

leaky roof."

"This is a terrible house!"
yelled Roddy. "There are no
toilets!"

"Don't be silly," said

Peter. "They are coming. My

dad never forgets anything."

Chapter 3
The New Homeowner

"I hope they paint the walls pink and blue," said JoJo. "Those colors are cheerful."

"Black is better," joked Pedro. "You can't see the dirt!"

"I want blue in the bedroom," said Miss Winkle. "And yellow in the kitchen."

"That sounds terrific," said Katie. "But the person who lives here will decide."

"Guess what?" said Miss Winkle. "I am that person! Mr. Patel is building this house for me."

"Wow!" said Katie. "Lucky you!"

"I'd like to see your house when it's finished," said JoJo. "With toilets and everything!" yelled Roddy.

"You will all see it!"

said Miss Winkle. "I'm

inviting the class to my

housewarming party."

"Wowzee!" yelled Katie.

A few weeks later, the house was ready. It was bright and cozy.

Katie and Pedro and JoJo gave Miss Winkle flowers.

Miss Winkle smiled even more when Mr. Patel and Peter gave her a cake.

What did the cake say?

"WELCOME HOME!"

Glossary

carpenter (KAR-puhn-ter)—a person who builds or repairs things made out of wood

concrete (KON-kreet)—a mixture of cement, water, sand, and gravel that hardens when it dries

digger (DIG-er)—a construction vehicle that digs holes

foundation (foun-DAY-shuhn)—a base on which something rests or is built

shingle (SHING-guhl)—a small, thin piece of building material that is placed in rows that overlap to cover and protect the roof of a building

tepee (TEE-pee)—a cone shaped tent, often made from animal skins and used as a home especially by Native nations in the Great Plains of the United States

terrific (tuh-RIF-ik)—unusually good

yurt (YURT)—a round tent made of animal skins or felt and used by nomads in central Asia

Katie's Questions

1. What traits make a good builder? Would you like to be a builder? Why or why not?

2. Draw a picture of your dream house. Then write one or two sentences to describe it.

3. Make a list of tools a builder might use. How many tools can you list?

4. Miss Winkle chose the paint colors for her house. If you were painting your bedroom, what color would you choose and why? Write a paragraph.

5. Make Miss Winkle a card to celebrate her new home. Be sure to write her a special message.

Katie Interviews a Builder

Katie: Mr. Patel, it was so much fun to learn about building houses. What is your favorite part about your job?

Mr. Patel: Do you ever build things from blocks? Isn't it cool to see how you can combine those materials to make something new? That's my favorite part about building. I can take wood and stone and nails and other materials and create a house from those items. That feels really good.

Katie: You work with a lot of sharp tools and big equipment. Do you ever worry about getting hurt?

Mr. Patel: Well, I am careful with the equipment I use, and I have special training so I know how to use the tools properly. Accidents can still happen, of course, but we work hard to stay safe.

Katie: How do you stay safe?

Mr. Patel: We wear hard hats to protect our heads and goggles to keep things from flying into our eyes when we use certain tools. We also wear sturdy boots to keep our feet safe, and earplugs to protect our hearing. We also have safety rules that everyone must follow.

Katie: How did you learn to be a builder?

Mr. Patel: I went to a trade school, which is a school that teaches skills for certain jobs, like construction or building. After I completed my classes, I took a special test to get my builder's license. I needed my license to build houses for other people.

Katie: Well, I bet Miss Winkle is happy you got your license! She loves her house.

Mr. Patel: I'm so happy about that. Miss Winkle deserves a beautiful home, don't you think?

Katie: I do! Thanks for talking to me today, Mr. Patel.

Mr. Patel: You are welcome, Katie Woo!

About the Author

Fran Manushkin is the author of Katie Woo, the highly acclaimed fan-favorite early reader series, as well as the popular Pedro series. Her other books include *Happy in Our Skin*, *Baby, Come Out!* and the best-selling board books *Big Girl Panties* and *Big Boy Underpants*. There is a real Katie Woo: Fran's great-niece, who doesn't get into trouble like the Katie in the books. Fran lives in New York City, three blocks from Central Park, where she can often be found bird-watching and daydreaming. She writes at her dining room table, without the help of her two naughty cats, Chaim and Goldy.

About the Illustrator

Laura Zarrin spent her early childhood in the St. Louis, Missouri, area. There she explored creeks, woods, and attic closets, climbed trees, and dug for artifacts in the backyard, all in preparation for her future career as an archaeologist. She never became one, however, because she realized she's much happier drawing in the comfort of her own home while watching TV. When she was twelve, her family moved to the Silicon Valley in California, where she still lives with her very logical husband and teen sons, and their illogical dog, Cody.